You're a Crab!

A Moody Day Book

Jenny Whitehead

Christy Ottaviano Books
Henry Holt and Company
New York

Wheeeeeee

Some days
you can be a
FRIENDLY
dolphin
with a
squeeeaky laugh.

Some days you can be
a **funny**
clownfish
that flips and does
somersaults.

Some days you can be a <u>silly</u> *jelly fish* that does a wiggle-jiggle dance.

When you feel
MAD
like an eel that
ZAPS
at whatever
it sees . . .

or **MEAN**
like a shark that wants
to CHOMP
on something squishy. . .

Duck,
Starfish!

or
frustrated
like a turtle
that SNAPs
at his lunch
(but misses),

then you are a CRAB—
a hard-shelled, sand-in-your-claws
crabby CRAB!

Don't worry. Sometimes I can be a crabby crab, too.

But not <u>TODAY!</u>
Today I'm a frog that goes

Kissy-Kissy-
Kissy!

I'm a minnow that wants to *tickle* your toes!

I'm a puffer fish that
will hold its breath
and make silly
faces at you.

and you want everyone to
LEAVE YOU ALONE,

or a mopey manatee,

or a squid
with a long face.

And when you're hungry,
tired, and irritable and
feel like blowing your top,
be a whale.

But if you don't . . .
how about I'll be a sea lion
and you be a sea horse,
and we can play ball?

Would you like to
tap-tap-toss
with your tail
while I bump-bump-bat
with my nose?

Or I can be a sawfish and you can be a hammerhead shark, and we can build something fun.

Would you like to hammer-hammer-hammer while I saw-saw-saw?

Or I can be an octopus and
you can be a sponge, and then
I would have eight arms

to hug You

and hug You

and SQueeZe You

and SQueeZe You

and hug You

and SQueeZe You

and hug you

and squeeze you.

(Maybe I'll go ahead and
do that anyway.)

But on
really
tough days,
when you're not
in the mood
to play
at all,

you can be a hermit crab,
and I can be a
hermit crab.

And we can sit in our shells
side by side in the sand
until you feel better.

You can take as long as you need
because I will be right here.

And soon enough . . .
you will be my happy,
funny, silly crab again!

FOR MY Chelsea x.o

Henry Holt and Company, LLC
Publishers since 1866
175 Fifth Avenue
New York, New York 10010
mackids.com

Henry Holt® is a registered trademark of Henry Holt and Company, LLC.
Copyright © 2015 by Jenny Whitehead
All rights reserved.

Library of Congress Cataloging-in-Publication Data
Whitehead, Jenny, author, illustrator.
You're a crab! : a moody day book / Jenny Whitehead. — First edition.
pages   cm
Summary: A little crab is in a bad mood, but his mother assures him that everyone feels
a bit crabby at times, and that when his mood changes they will have all sorts of fun.
ISBN 978-0-8050-9361-2 (hardback)
[1. Mood (Psychology)—Fiction. 2. Friendship—Fiction. 3. Crabs—Fiction.
4. Marine animals—Fiction.] I. Title. II. Title: You are a crab!
PZ7.1.W45You 2015   [E]—dc23   2014031096

Henry Holt books may be purchased for business or promotional use. For information
on bulk purchases, please contact Macmillan Corporate and Premium Sales Department
at (800) 221-7945 x5442 or by e-mail at specialmarkets@macmillan.com.

First Edition—2015
The artist used tissue paper, paint, and Photoshop to create the illustrations for this book.

Printed in China by South China Printing Co. Ltd., Dongguan City, Guangdong Province
1 3 5 7 9 10 8 6 4 2

He sure was
a hard shell
to crack today!

Hee
hee-
yep!